W9-BWD-635

FROG KNOWS BEST

All inquiries should be addressed to:
Barron's Educational Series, Inc.
250 Wireless Boulevard
Hauppauge, NY 11788

International Standard Book Number 0-8120-4855-5

Library of Congress Catalog Card Number 91-39903

Library of Congress Cataloging-in-Publication Data

Foster, Kelli C.
   Frog knows best / by Foster & Erickson; illustrations by Kerri Gifford.
   p. cm. (Get ready—get set—read!)
   Summary: A frog in a bog tries to give advice to two joggers
about the dangers of jogging in the fog.
ISBN 0-8120-4855-5
   (1. Frogs—Fiction.   2. Bogs—Fiction.   3. Running—Fiction.
4. Stories in rhyme.)
I. Erickson, Gina Clegg. II. Russell, Kerri Gifford, ill. III. Title. IV. Series:
Erickson, Gina Clegg. Get ready—get set—read!
PZ8.3.F813Fr 1992
(E)—dc20   91-39903
                                               CIP
                                               AC

PRINTED IN HONG KONG
20 19 18 17 16

GET READY...GET SET...READ!

FROG KNOWS BEST

by
Foster & Erickson

Illustrations by
Kerri Gifford Russell

BARRON'S

T. J. Frog sits by the bog.

A log is in the bog.

A dog and a hog
jog around the bog.

"Don't jog by the bog,"
says T. J. Frog.

"We know best," says the ho
So on they jog.

Fog comes to the bog.

"Don't jog in the fog,"
says T. J. Frog.

We know best," says the hog.
o on they jog.

The dog and hog
fall in the bog.
Slog, slog.

"Get on that log,"
says the hog.

"Not **that** log!"
calls T. J. Frog.

"We know best," says the hog.
So they get on the log.

The two sit on the log.

"This is not a log.
Run!" says the hog.

"I think the frog knows best,"
says the dog.

The End

The OG Word Family

bog
dog
fog
frog
hog
jog
log
slog

Sight Words

so
don't
fall
know
knows
says
they
calls
think
around

Dear Parents and Educators:

Welcome to *Get Ready...Get Set...Read!*

We've created these books to introduce children to the magic of reading.

Each story in the series is built around one or two word families. For example, *A Mop for Pop* uses the OP word family. Letters and letter blends are added to OP to form words such as TOP, LOP, and STOP. As you can see, once children are able to read OP, it is a simple task for them to read the entire word family. In addition to word families, we have used a limited number of "sight words." These are words found to occur with high frequency in the books your child will soon be reading. Being able to identify sight words greatly increases reading skill.

You might find the steps outlined on the facing page useful in guiding your work with your beginning reader.

We had great fun creating these books, and great pleasure sharing them with our children. We hope *Get Ready...Get Set...Read!* helps make this first step in reading fun for you and your new reader.

Kelli C. Foster, PhD
Educational Psychologist

Gina Clegg Erickson, MA
Reading Specialist

Guidelines for Using *Get Ready...Get Set...Read!*

Step 1.   Read the story to your child.

Step 2.   Have your child read the Word Family list aloud several times.

Step 3.   Invent new words for the list. Print each new combination for your child to read. Remember, nonsense words can be used (*dat, kat, gat*).

Step 4.   Read the story *with* your child. He or she reads all of the Word Family words; you read the rest.

Step 5.   Have your child read the Sight Word list aloud several times.

Step 6.   Read the story *with* your child again. This time he or she reads the words from both lists; you read the rest.

Step 7.   Your child reads the entire book to you!

Titles in the

Series:

SET 1

Find Nat
The Sled Surprise
Sometimes I Wish
A Mop for Pop
The Bug Club
BRING-IT-ALL-TOGETHER BOOKS
What a Day for Flying!
Bat's Surprise

SET 2

The Tan Can
The Best Pets Yet
Pip and Kip
Frog Knows Best
Bub and Chub
BRING-IT-ALL-TOGETHER BOOKS
Where Is the Treasure?
What a Trip!

SET 3

Jake and the Snake
Jeepers Creepers
Two Fine Swine
What Rose Does Not Know
Pink and Blue
BRING-IT-ALL-TOGETHER BOOKS
The Pancake Day
Hide and Seek

SET 4

Whiptail of Blackshale Trail
Colleen and the Bean
Dwight and the Trilobite
The Old Man at the Moat
By the Light of the Moon
BRING-IT-ALL-TOGETHER BOOKS
Night Light
The Crossing

SET 5

Tall and Small
Bounder's Sound
How to Catch a Butterfly
Ludlow Grows Up
Matthew's Brew
BRING-IT-ALL-TOGETHER BOOKS
Snow in July
Let's Play Ball